THE BREAD AND THE WINE

The Story of the Last Supper

The Last Supper, John 13:1-38, 1 Corinthians 11:23-34 FOR CHILDREN

Written by Denise Ahern
Illustrated by Alice Hausner

ARCH® Books

MANUFACTURED IN THE UNITED STATES OF AMERICA

ISBN 0-570-06127-X

Ben loved to play in his large house
a game of hide and seek.
He had a special, secret place
where he alone could peek.

A tiny closet, dark and snug,
where jars and bowls were stored,
was where he'd sit; his eyes shone bright
through a crack in the closet door.

One day he heard his mother say
that guests would soon arrive,
so up the stairs he rapidly raced
and hid where he could spy.

Two men walked in, their arms heaped high
with baskets, jars, and bowls.
They set the table, then neatly placed
bright pillows in two rows.

A delicious smell filled the room,
of roasted lamb and bread;
in walked Ben's mother with the food.
"We're ready to dine," they said.

On the stairs Ben heard footsteps;
a crowd of friends came in.
Around the table each took his place;
Ben counted 13 men.

They started then to sing a song;
the man in the center beamed—
But one man wore a tight-lipped frown.
Ben thought, "He sure looks mean."

The leader rose, He tucked His robe,
poured water from a vase,
and set the bowl upon the floor.

A smile played on His face.
Then like a servant He dipped a towel
and went down to His knees.

"That's Jesus," Ben stared in surprise,
"I heard the people sing
that day when He rode through the streets
'Hosannah to the King!'

"If He is King, He should not wash
their feet, that's servant's work."
Jesus explained, "As I have done,
each other you must serve."

Then Jesus sat and prayed, "Dear God,
please bless this Passover meal."
They feasted on the lamb and bread,
began to eat their fill.

Ben thought of Passover, the very first—
God's people, the Jews, each chose
a lamb with wool so soft and white,
the one they loved the most.

They spread its blood upon their door
so God would keep them safe
and lead them from the land of Egypt
where they worked hard as slaves.

Jesus was silent; tears filled His eyes.
Ben thought, "He looks so sad."
His friends whispered, "What is wrong?
Let's try to make Him glad."

They thought of the past and Peter said,
"Remember that time at sea?
I walked to meet You on the water
but sank up to my knees!"
Jesus smiled—a tender smile,
"You've learned a lot since then."
"They love Jesus so much," Ben thought
"They really are good friends."

Ben listened; Jesus softly spoke,
"My betrayer is here this night."
Wonderingly, the 12 men stared;
each asked, "Lord, is it I?"

Beside Jesus sat one man;
his eyes were wide with fear.
Trembling he whispered, "Is it I?"
Ben strained hard to hear.

A man named John leaned toward Jesus,
"Who is it, Lord?" he said.
Jesus slowly turned and gave
the frightened man His bread.

"Judas, go," then Jesus spoke,
"and do what must be done."
With scowling brow, Judas fled;
Ben said, "I'm glad he's gone!"

Jesus sighed a deep, long sigh;
His face was very grave.
He broke in half a loaf of bread
and bowed His head to pray.

"Take and eat; this is My body,
given for your sins."
Jesus passed the bread around
to each one of His friends.

Ben thought, "The other day I tied
a rock to my cat's tail;
she spun around, jumped on the table—
then crash—a clay pot fell!

My mother says that it is sin
when I do what is bad.
All the men seem so unhappy;
for sin makes Jesus sad."

Then Jesus took a cup of wine.
Ben thought, "What will He do?"
Jesus said, "This is God's new covenant
sealed with My blood, shed for you.
Do this to remember Me.
Drink this cup of Mine."
Ben watched as each man raised the cup
and tasted the sweet wine.

All the men joined in to sing
a song in closing prayer.
Their voices rang in highest praise
that burst the still night air.

Quietly they left the room;
Ben heard their footsteps echo
on the stairs and through the streets
as after Him they followed.

Ben sat alone; the room was dark;
but he was not afraid.
He still could see the gentle eyes,
the smile on Jesus' face.

Scooting from his hiding place,
he felt so stiff and sore.
He quickly ran from the room
and quietly shut the door.

Just then he heard his mother call,
"Where are you, Benjamin?"
Running down the stairs, he knew
Jesus would be *his* Friend.

DEAR PARENT:

A rereading of the story of the Last Supper brings to the minds of most readers the painting by Leonardo da Vinci on the wall of the Convent of Santa Maria delle Grazie. In the fresco, a classical example of Renaissance design, all focuses on Christ. The vanishing point in the perspective of the picture is in the face of Christ. The mood is set. Christ would be alone in His suffering: No one would stand by Him or be ready to die with Him. We read of His last words and know how His life will end.

Yet the story of the Last Supper is prefaced in John 13:1 with these words: "Jesus . . . having loved His own who were in the world, He loved them to the end (RSV). Nothing is so constant as Christ's love and faithfulness. We read of the foot washing, of Judas' betrayal, of Christ's agony to pay for the sins of all mankind. But still through all Christ's love persists.

Explain to your child the meaning and history of God's covenant. Tell him often of the love of Christ, and try to teach, by word and example, the lifestyle of Christian love.

THE EDITOR